I WISH I'D SAILED WITH CAPTAIN COOK

Written by
LEONIE YOUNG

Illustrated by
TOHBY RIDDLE

WELDON KIDS

Published in Australia by
Weldon Kids Pty Ltd
Unit 4, 9 Apollo Street
Warriewood NSW 2102 Australia
A member of the Weldon
International Group of Companies

First published 1993
Reprinted 1997, 2001

Publishing Director: Leonie Weldon
Editor: Avril Janks
Project Co-ordinator: Leah Walsh
Production Manager: Cathy Wadling
Designer: Stan Lamond
Printed in China through
Jade Productions

© Weldon Kids Pty Ltd

National Library of Australia
Cataloguing-in-Publication Data
Young, Leonie
I wish I'd sailed with Captain Cook.
ISBN 1 86302 163 9. H/B
ISBN 1 86302 183 3. P/B
1. Cook, James, 1728-1779 --
Journeys -- Juvenile fiction.
1. Title.
A823.3

Dedicated to
Jason, Peter and Michael

The author would like to thank the following people:
Robert Coupe, Stuart Glover and Sally Gavin

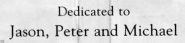

I wish I'd sailed with Captain Cook!

A long time ago in faraway England there lived a boy named James Cook. He worked hard at school and in his spare time would help his father work on a farm.

James was always dreaming of an adventurous life and of going to far-distant places.

When he was old enough, James went to work in a grocery shop that sold tea and sugar and flour and delicious things to eat.

But he still dreamed of the adventurous life.

One day, the captain of a ship came into the shop and asked him if he would like to learn to be a sailor. James couldn't wait to start!

The ship carried cargoes of coal to ports up and down the English coast and there was a lot to learn about sailing.

James learnt to climb the masts and set the sails.

He learnt how to steer the ship.

He learnt how to scrub the decks.

And how to paint and caulk the ship's side so it wouldn't leak.

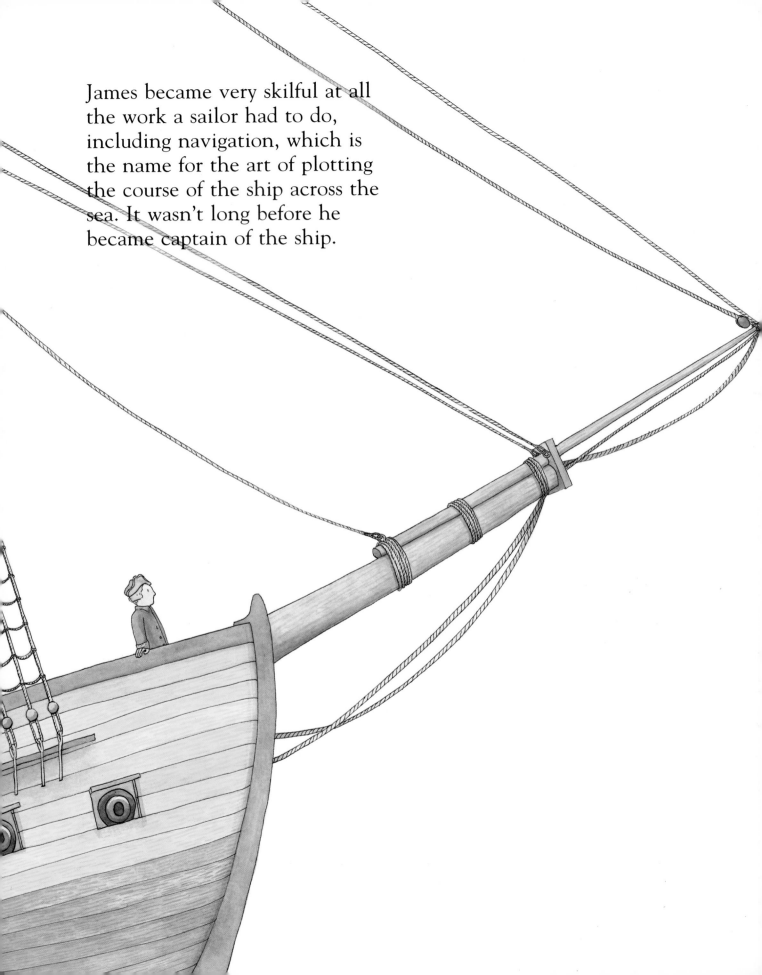

James became very skilful at all the work a sailor had to do, including navigation, which is the name for the art of plotting the course of the ship across the sea. It wasn't long before he became captain of the ship.

James captained many ships, including ships in the King's navy, until one day he was chosen to be the captain on a very special voyage of discovery. This was to be his greatest adventure.

There was a group of very important men who worked for the King. They were called The Royal Society, and their job was to get people to go exploring so they could learn more about the world.

They told James to get a ship ready to sail to the furthest places on the most distant oceans. They handed him an envelope containing secret instructions, so secret that even he was not to open the envelope until he was far out to sea.

King George III gave James a ship, and it was named the *Endeavour*.

On board were 71 crewmen, 12 sea-going soldiers (called marines) to protect the ship and crew, and 9 naturalists. Their job was discovering any new, strange plants, animals and places on the journey.

When the *Endeavour* departed, a huge crowd gathered to wish them farewell on their historic voyage.

SEXTANT

Soon the *Endeavour* was far out to sea. There was no land anywhere in sight. This was where Captain James Cook's famous skills in navigation were called upon.

Using the ship's compass, James was able to keep his ship sailing in the right direction.

With an instrument called a sextant, he used the planets and stars by night and the sun by day to find exactly where his ship was on the great empty oceans.

For months and months they sailed on.

During the voyage, the *Endeavour* visited many strange and
wonderful places that were very different to anything back home.
They saw Rio de Janeiro and Tierra del Fuego, one near the top of
South America and the other right at the bottom.

One of Captain Cook's favourite places was a beautiful island
called Tahiti. It had high mountains and beaches with waving
palm trees.

The people of Tahiti were excellent surfers. They also danced a
lot, and had races in their canoes.

Captain Cook had important work to do in Tahiti. He had to study the planet Venus. One day that year, it would move in front of the sun for just a few minutes.

Finding out all about this would help other captains navigate, using the planets, sun and stars.

One night, not long after leaving Tahiti, Captain Cook knew the time had come to break the seal, and opened his secret orders. He read: 'You must search for a land called Terra Australis. We believe it's somewhere in the vast ocean to the south of the equator.'

James was very excited and sailed on, determined to find the mysterious Terra Australis. He sailed right around New Zealand as he searched.

How far Terra Australis was no one could really be sure, and life could be quite boring for the sailors and marines on the ship. Some days passed very slowly.

Sailing a ship on the seas could also be very dangerous.
There were fierce storms, when huge waves came crashing onto the deck and the sailors had to work day and night to keep the ship from sinking.

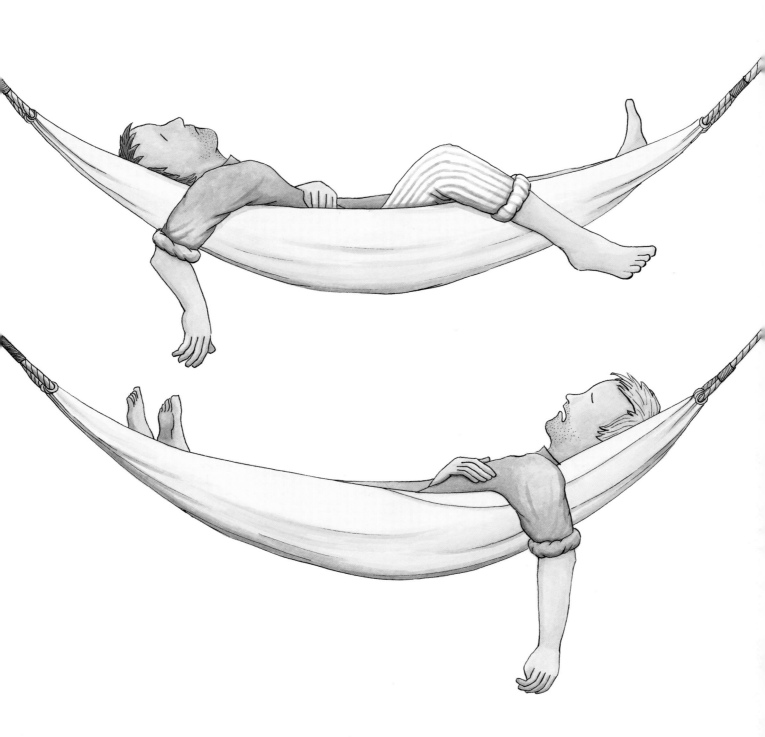

Sometimes it was terribly hot, and sometimes it was very cold.
Some of the people on the ship got very sick.

Just when some of the crew and some of the marines and naturalists were thinking there could be no such place as Terra Australis ...

... a sailor who was high up on the mast shouted, 'Land ahoy! Land ahoy!'

This was a very exciting moment for everyone on board.

Captain Cook could see thick forests and long white beaches and pillars of smoke rising from among the trees. He knew this meant there were people living in the forests. They were probably cooking their dinners over campfires.

Captain Cook sailed the *Endeavour* up the coast, searching for a safe place to anchor.

Through a wide inlet there seemed to be a perfect place. It was a huge stretch of calm water.

Captain Cook named the place Botany Bay. And there they dropped the anchor and rolled up the sails.

Then they rowed ashore in the ship's boats.

The Aborigines who lived on the land had never seen such a big ship before. They had never seen white men before either.

All of the people from the ship wanted to learn about this strange country.

Captain Cook went for a long walk in the bush and wrote about everything he saw in his log book.

Nobody from the *Endeavour* had ever seen plants and animals that looked like these—the birds were beautifully coloured and the plants were very unusual. The naturalists couldn't wait to draw the incredible creatures they saw.

The mysterious land—Terra Australis—that Captain Cook discovered is now called Australia.

People from many different lands have come to live there.

Now there are big cities.

There are lots of houses.

There are roads everywhere and thousands of cars.

If Captain Cook could see Australia now, he would be very surprised, wouldn't he?